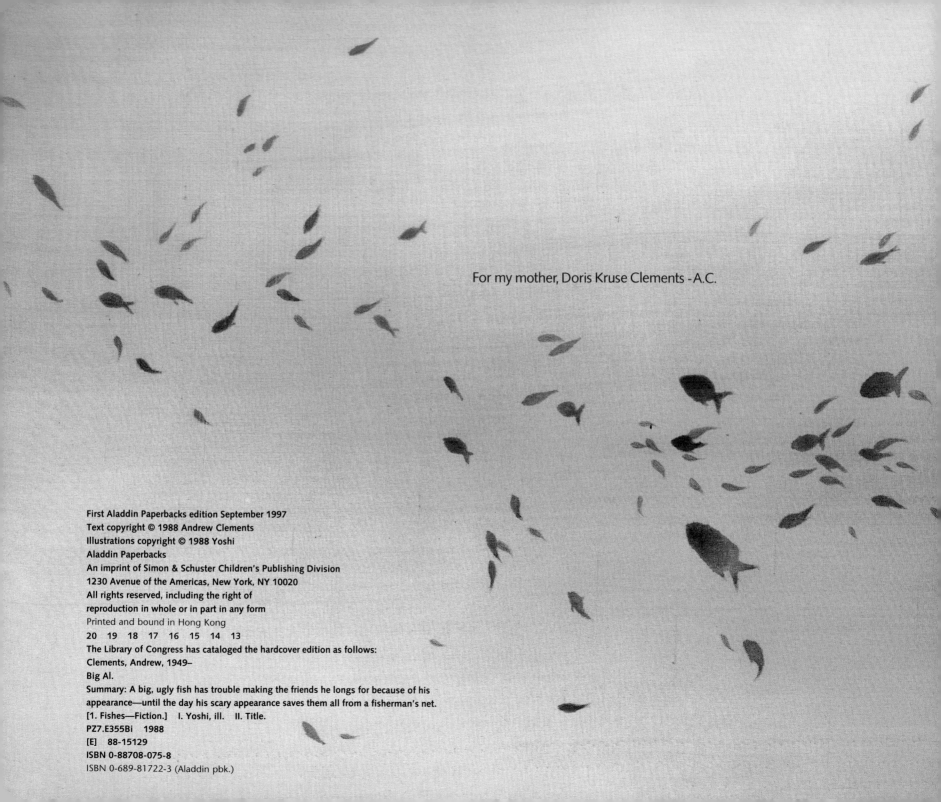

For my mother, Doris Kruse Clements -A.C.

First Aladdin Paperbacks edition September 1997
Text copyright © 1988 Andrew Clements
Illustrations copyright © 1988 Yoshi
Aladdin Paperbacks
An imprint of Simon & Schuster Children's Publishing Division
1230 Avenue of the Americas, New York, NY 10020
Printed and bound in Hong Kong
20   19   18   17   16   15   14   13
The Library of Congress has cataloged the hardcover edition as follows:
Clements, Andrew, 1949–
Big Al.
Summary: A big, ugly fish has trouble making the friends he longs for because of his
appearance—until the day his scary appearance saves them all from a fisherman's net.
[1. Fishes—Fiction.]   I. Yoshi, ill.   II. Title.
PZ7.E355Bi   1988
[E]   88-15129
ISBN 0-88708-075-8
ISBN 0-689-81722-3 (Aladdin pbk.)

BIG AL

Yoshi

Andrew Clements

Aladdin Paperbacks

In the wide blue sea there was a very friendly fish named Big Al.
You could not find a nicer fish.

But Big Al was also very,

very,

scary.

Other fish seemed to have at least one friend. Some had many. But Big Al had none.

He did not really blame the other fish. How could he expect **little** fish to trust a great **big** fish with eyes and skin and TEETH like his?

So Big Al was lonely, and cried big salty tears into the big salty sea.

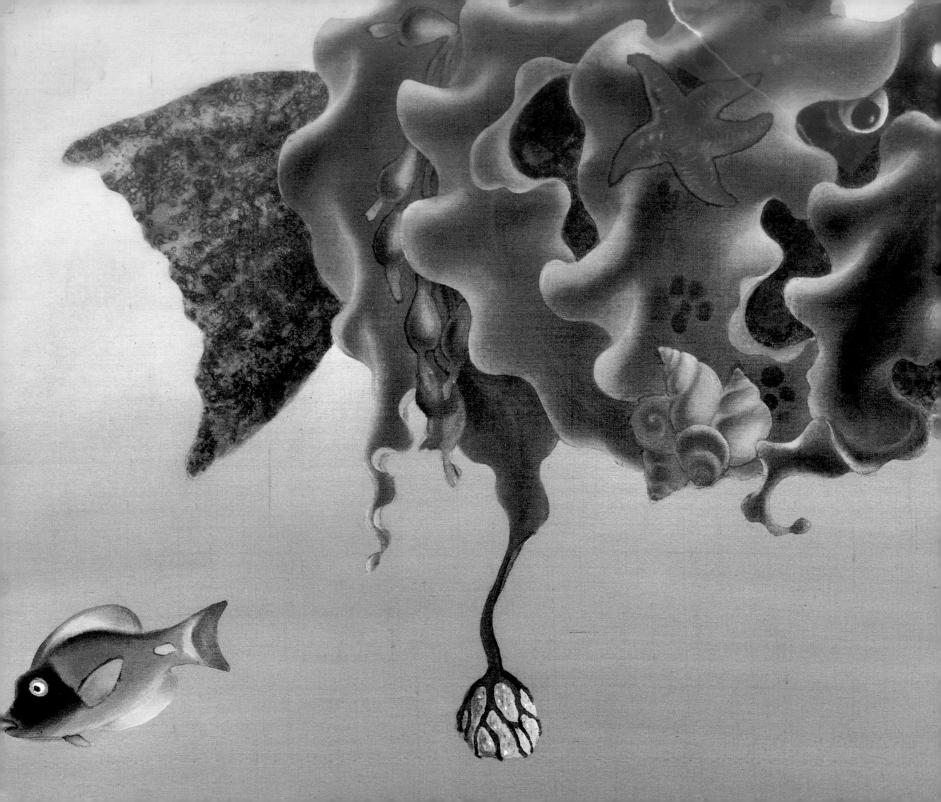

But Big Al really wanted friends, so he worked at it.

First he tried wrapping himself up with seaweed. He thought it was a great disguise, but no one else did. Who wants to stop and talk to a floating plant that has big sharp teeth?

Then he thought that if he puffed himself up round, the other fish would laugh, and see how clever and silly he could be.

All they saw was how BIG he could be, and they steered clear.

Very early one morning, Big Al
went down to the bottom and
flopped and wiggled himself into
the sand until he was almost covered up.
He looked much smaller. When other fish came near,
Big Al talked and joked with them and had a delightful time.
But then one scratchy little grain of sand got stuck in his gills—
and he…and hehe…and he sn…and he SSSNEEEEEEZED.

When the clouds of sand cleared away,
all the other fish were gone.

Big Al even changed his color one day so he could look like he belonged to a school of tiny fish passing by. He bubbled along with them for a while, laughing and feeling like he was just one of the crowd.

But he was so big and clumsy that when all the tiny fish darted to the left and then quickly back to the right, Big Al just plowed straight ahead. He went bumping and thumping right into the little fish. Before he could even say "Excuse me," they were gone, and he was all alone again, sadder than ever.

Just when Big Al was starting to be sure that he would never have a single friend, something happened.

He was floating along sadly watching some of the smaller fish, and was wishing they would come closer. As he watched, a net dropped down silently from above, and in an instant, they were caught.

Big Al forgot all about being lonely, and he
forgot all about being sad. His eyes bulged
out bigger and rounder than ever, and
with a mighty flip of his tail he opened
his mouth and charged straight at
the net! The net was strong,
but Big Al was stronger.
He ripped right through it,
and all the little fish rushed
out through the hole.

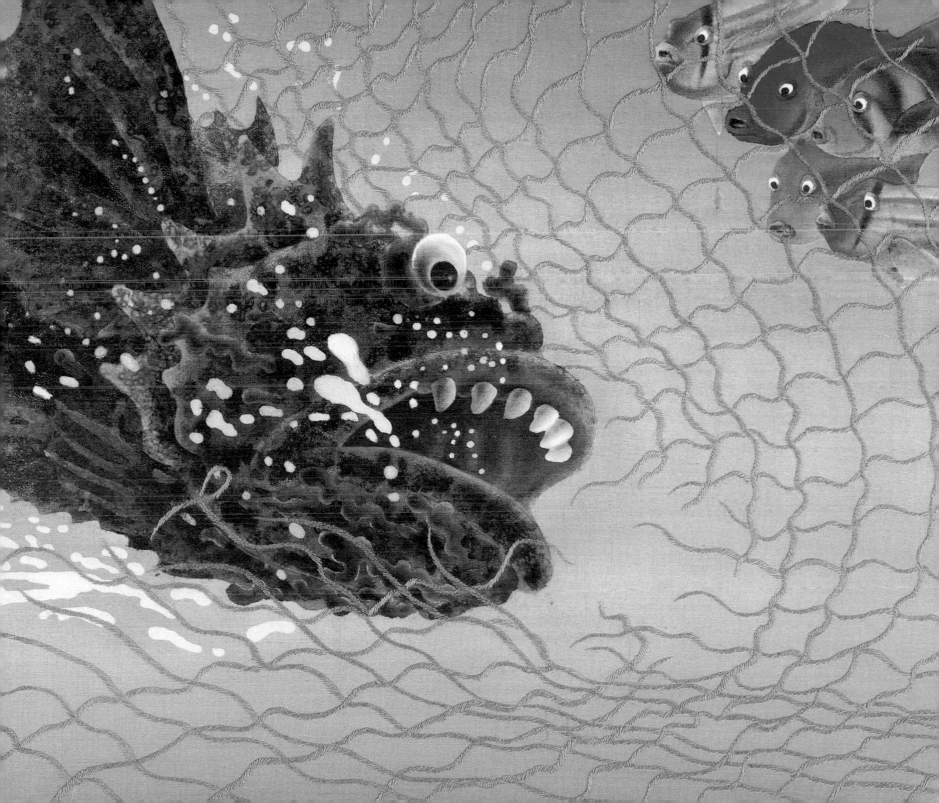

But when Big Al tried to turn around and go out of the hole, he got all tangled up in the net. He was stuck!

The net went higher and higher toward the bright
surface of the sea, and the little fish watched
Big Al as he disappeared above them.

When the little fish were able to speak again, all
they talked about was the huge, wonderful fish that
had saved them. How great to be free, but what
a shame that the big fellow had been captured.

Just then there was a tremendous, crashing splash above them, and the small fish dashed away. Was it the net again?

Not at all—It was Big Al. Those fishermen took one look at him, and threw him right back into the ocean.

And now there is one huge, puffy, scary, fierce-looking fish in the sea who has more friends than anyone else:

Big Al.